Thank you to the generous team who _
talents to make this book possible:

Author
Jane Kurtz

Illustrators
Caroline Greger, Margi Brown, Rowan Schmitt,
Students from Findley Elementary School, Judah Gerards

Creative directors
Caroline Kurtz and Jane Kurtz

Translator
Amlaku B. Eshetie

Designer
Beth Crow

Ready Set Go Books, an Open Hearts Big Dreams Project

Special thanks to Ethiopia Reads donors and staff for
believing in this project and helping get it started-- and
for arranging printing, distribution, and training in Ethiopia.

8/18/18

Football Fun

የእግር ኳስ ጨዋታ

English and Amharic

We all play ball.

ኳስ እንጫወታለን።

We play in the grass.

በሳር ላይ እንጫወታለን።

We play on the street.

በመንገድ ላይ እንጫወታለን።

We are clever with
our feet.

እግሮቻችን ቀልጣፊች
ናቸው።

After school we race to play.

ከት/ቤት በኋላ
ለመጫወት
እንራራጣለን።

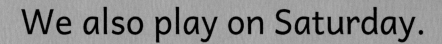

We also play on Saturday.

ቅዳሜ-ቅዳሜም እንጫወታለን።

We make
teams.

We like to pass the spinning ball through the grass.

በሳሩ ላይ
የምትሽከረከረውን ኳስ
መለጋት እንወዳለን።

Sometimes we have no ball for play.

አንዳንድ ጊዜ የምንጫወትበት ኳስ አይኖረንም።

We can make
one anyway.

እንደምንም ብለን ግን
አንድ አናጣም።

We all
play ball.

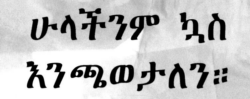

ሁላችንም ኳስ
እንጫወታለን።

We steal.

ከተጋጣሚ ተጫዋች እንቀማለን፨

We block. እንከላከላለን።

We run.

እንሮጣለን።

We stop.

እንቆማለን።

We score!

ግብ እናስገባለን!

About The Story

Many Ethiopians describe themselves as "football fanatics." The country's national team, the Walia Antelopes, was organized in 1943 and played its first competition in 1947, one of the first to take part in international competition in Africa. In 1957, the team finished second in the African Nations Cup. As many as 35,000 screaming fans sometimes fill Addis Ababa Stadium, and a new FIFA standard stadium will be able to hold 60,000 fans. But the children of Ethiopia—as this book shows—play soccer/football anywhere they can!

Some illustrations in this book show the One World Futbol that "never needs a pump and never goes flat" (https://www.oneworldplayproject.com). Many American tourists and volunteers have put those blue futbols in their luggage to donate to kids in Ethiopia because they agree with the founder of that project: "Play is in our DNA—a need as important as food, medicine and shelter."

About the Author

Jane Kurtz learned to read in Maji, Ethiopia. Many years later, she helped start the not-for-profit Ethiopia Reads, hoping to share book love with young readers in Ethiopia and her own Ethiopian-American grandchildren. She has published almost forty books for young readers and is on the faculty of the Vermont College of Fine Arts MFA in Children's and Young Adult Literature. Jane has volunteered with Ethiopia Reads for almost twenty years and now is part of the team creating Ready Set Go Books.

About The Illustrators

In 2017, Westminster Presbyterian Church in Portland, Oregon held an art making day for Ready Set Go books where both adults and young artists worked on illustrating this story, including one of the youngest artists (Rowan Schmitt) to have her work included in a Ready Set Go book.

About Ready Set Go Books

Reading has the power to change lives, but many children and adults in Ethiopia cannot read. One reason is that Ethiopia has very few books in local languages to give people a chance to practice reading. Ready Set Go books wants to close that gap and open a world of ideas and possibilities for kids and their communities.

When you buy a Ready Set Go book, you provide critical funding to create and distribute more books.

Learn more at: http://openheartsbigdreams.org/book-project/

About Ethiopia Reads

Ethiopia Reads was started by volunteers in places like Grand Forks, North Dakota; Denver, Colorado; San Francisco, California; and Washington D.C. who wanted to give the gift of reading to more kids in Ethiopia.

One of the founders, Jane Kurtz, learned to read in Ethiopia where she spent most of her childhood and where the circle of life has come around to bring her Ethiopian-American grandchildren. As a children's book author, Jane is the driving force behind Ready Set Go Books - working to create the books that inspire those just learning to read.

About Open Hearts Big Dreams

Open Hearts Big Dreams began as a volunteer organization, led by Ellenore Angelidis in Seattle, Washington, to provide sustainable funding and strategic support to Ethiopia reads, collaborating with Jane Kurtz. OHBD has now grown to be its own nonprofit organization supporting literacy, art, and technology for young people in Ethiopia.

Ellenore comes from a family of teachers who believe education is a human right, and opportunity should not depend on your birthplace. And as the adoptive mother of a little girl who was born in Ethiopia and learned to read in the U.S., as well as an aspiring author, she finds the chance to positively impact literacy hugely compelling!

About the Language

Amharic is a Semetic language -- in fact, the world's second-most widely spoken Semetic language, after Arabic. Starting in the 12th century, it became the Ethiopian language that was used in official transactions and schools and became widely spoken all over Ethiopia. It's written with its own characters, over 260 of them. Eritrea and Ethiopia share this alphabet, and they are the only countries in Africa to develop a writing system centuries ago that is still in use today!

About the Translation

Translation is currently being coordinated by a volunteer, Amlaku Bikss Eshetie who has a BA degree in Foreign Languages & Literature, an MA in Teaching English as a Foreign Language, and PhD courses in Applied Linguistics and Communication, all at Addis Ababa University. He taught English from elementary through university levels and is currently a passionate and experienced English-Amharic translator. As a father of three, he also has a special interest in child literacy and development. He can be reached at: khaabba_ils@protonmail.com

Find more Ready Set Go Books on Amazon.com

To view all available titles, search "Ready Set Go Ethiopia" or scan QR code

 Chaos

 Talk Talk Turtle

 The Glory of Gondar

 We Can Stop the Lion

 Not Ready!

 Fifty Lemons

Made in the USA
Middletown, DE
28 February 2019